Pork and Beans:
Play Date

by JOVIAL BOB STINE

illustrated by JOSE ARUEGO and ARIANE DEWEY

SCHOLASTIC HARDCOVER

SCHOLASTIC INC.

New York   Toronto   London   Auckland   Sydney

Library of Congress Cataloging-in-Publication Data
Stine, Jovial Bob.
Pork and beans: play date/by Jovial Bob Stine; illustrated by
Jose Aruego and Ariane Dewey.
p.   cm.
Summary: Pork and Beans spend a fun day playing with Billy and
making up games such as Bad Cold, Bump Tag, and Wagon Pull.
ISBN 0-590-41579-4
[1. Play—Fiction. 2. Games—Fiction.]   I. Aruego, Jose, ill.
II. Dewey, Ariane, ill.   III. Title.
PZ7.S8603Po 1989
[E]—dc19   88-18205
                                                      CIP
                                                       AC

12 11 10 9 8 7 6 5 4 3 2 1   9/8 0 1 2 3 4/9
Printed in the U.S.A.   36
First Scholastic printing, May 1989

For Matty
—J. B. S.

For Juan
—J. A. and A. D.

This is Pork.

And this is Beans.
They live in a little house on a big farm.

"Your friend Billy is coming to play with you today," says Mrs. Pig.

"Good," says Pork. "Billy is my best friend."
"Billy is my best friend, too," says Beans.
"No. Mine," says Pork.

"Don't fight," says Mrs. Pig. "Here comes Billy."

"Hi, Billy," says Pork. "You are my best friend."
"You are my best friend, too," says Beans.
"Henry is my best friend," says Billy. "Not you."
"We like Henry, too," says Beans.
"No," says Billy. "Henry is *my* friend. Not yours."
"Go play," says Mrs. Pig.

"Let's stay out and play," says Beans.
"I don't want to," says Billy.
"Then let's go in and play," says Pork.
"I don't want to," says Billy.

"What can we play?" asks Billy.
"I don't know," says Pork.
"Let's think," says Beans.
 They think and think.
"This is boring," says Billy.

"Let's play Bad Cold," says Beans. "Billy can be
   the doctor."
"How do you play Bad Cold?" asks Billy.
"We'll show you," says Pork.
"I'll go first," says Beans. He sneezes on Billy.
"Don't do that," says Billy.

"Doctor, I have a bad cold," says Beans.
He sneezes on Billy again.
"Stop," says Billy. "That's not nice."
"You are the doctor," says Pork.
Pork sneezes on Billy.
Then Beans sneezes on Billy.
Then Pork sneezes on Billy again.
"Stop it! Stop it!" says Billy.

Billy starts to cry.

"What are you doing?" asks Mrs. Pig.
"Pork and Beans sneezed on me," says Billy.
"It was just a game," says Beans.
"Play another game," says Mrs. Pig.

"Let's play Bump Tag," says Billy.

"What's that?" asks Beans. "How do you play?"

"I will show you," says Billy.

"You're *it*," Billy says to Beans.

"What does that mean?" asks Beans.

"You'll see," says Billy.

Billy runs at Beans. BUMP.
Beans falls down.
"Stop that!" says Beans.
Pork runs at Beans. BUMP.
Beans falls down again.
"Stop that," says Beans.

"You're *it*. You're still *it*!" says Billy.
BUMP.
Billy bumps Beans again.
BUMP.
Pork bumps Beans again.

Beans starts to cry.
"What are you doing?" asks Mrs. Pig.
"Billy and Pork bumped me," says Beans.
"We were playing Bump Tag," says Pork.
"It's a game I made up," says Billy.
"Play another game," says Mrs. Pig.

"Let's play Wagon Pull," says Beans.
"Yes," says Pork.
"How do you play Wagon Pull?" asks Billy.
"We'll show you," says Beans.
    Beans gets in the wagon. "Pull me," he says to Pork.

Pork pulls Beans. Beans has a long ride.
Then Billy gets in the wagon. "Pull me," he says.
Pork pulls Billy. Billy has a long ride.

Then Beans and Billy both get in the wagon.
"Pull us," they say.
Pork pulls Beans and Billy. They have a long ride.

Pork gets in the wagon. "Now pull me," says Pork.
"I can't," says Beans. "All that riding up and down in
the wagon made me too tired."
"I can't," says Billy. "I'm tired, too."

Pork starts to cry.

"What are you doing?" asks Mrs. Pig.

"They won't pull me," says Pork.

"I'm too tired," says Billy.

"We don't want to play Wagon Pull anymore," says Beans.

"Then play another game," says Mrs. Pig.

They play Catch the Corncob.
Beans throws the corncob to Billy.
Billy throws the corncob to Beans.
Beans throws the corncob to Billy.
Billy throws the corncob to Beans.

They play Squash the Bug.
Beans is the bug.

Pork sits on Beans.

Then Billy sits on Beans.

Then Pork and Billy
sit on Beans.
"Help!" says Beans.

"I don't like that game," says Beans.

"Okay. Let's play Snowman," says Pork. "Billy can be the snowman."

"But we don't have snow," says Beans.

"We can use mud," says Pork.

They put mud on Billy. Lots and lots of mud.

"Do I look like a snowman?" asks Billy.

"No," says Pork. "You look like a mess."

"You don't play fair!" cries Billy. "You're not nice, and you don't play nice games!"

"Billy, look who is here," says Mrs. Pig.
"Your mother has come for you."

Billy sees his mother. He starts to cry.

He cries and cries.

Pork and Beans start to cry.
Pork and Beans and Billy cry and cry.

"What is the matter?" asks Billy's mother.

"Why are you all so sad?"

"You came too soon!" cry Pork and Beans.

"I don't want to go home yet," cries Billy.

"We are having too much fun!"

"This was our best play date ever," cry Pork and Beans.

And they all cried and cried.